Dragon Tooth

Story and Pictures by
Cathryn Falwell

Clarion Books/New York

Clarion Books • a Houghton Mifflin Company imprint • 215 Park Avenue South, New York, NY 10003 • Text and illustrations copyright © 1996 by Cathryn Falwell • The illustrations for this book were executed in cut paper, including recycled scraps • The text is set in 18/26.5-point New Baskerville. • All rights reserved. • For information about permission to reproduce selections from this book, write to Permissions, Houghton Mifflin Company, 215 Park Avenue South, New York, NY 10003. • For information about this and other Houghton Mifflin trade and reference books and multimedia products, visit The Bookstore at Houghton Mifflin on the World Wide Web at (http://www.hmco.com/trade/). • Printed in the USA.

Library of Congress Cataloging-in-Publication Data

Falwell, Cathryn. • Dragon tooth / by Cathryn Falwell ; written and illustrated by Cathryn Falwell.
p.   cm. • Summary: When her father offers to pull her loose tooth, Sara has to adjust to the idea in her own way. • ISBN 0-395-56916-8 • [1. Teeth—Fiction.   2. Dragons—Fiction.]   I. Title.
PZ7.F198Dr • 1996 • [E]—dc20 • 95-35207 • CIP • AC
HOR   10   9   8   7   6   5   4   3   2   1

For the Dragon Builders
of Noah Webster School
and for
Axie, Krystal, Fionna, Keisha,
KitKat, Inelise, and Torrie:
Young women with spunk!

OOOOWWWW
oww
www

Sara's tooth
was loose.
It was very wobbly
and it hurt.
"Oooowwwwwww!"
Sara wailed.

"That tooth is
an old dragon
roaring in your
mouth," said Papa.
"Let me pull it out
for you."

"No!" said Sara.
"I don't want it
pulled. It hurts."

"Then why don't
you help me with
supper?" said Papa.
"If you think about
something else,
perhaps the dragon
will be quiet."

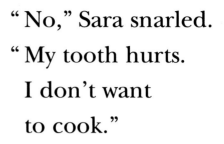

"No," Sara snarled.
"My tooth hurts.
I don't want
to cook."

"Sara," said Papa,
"your tooth is
loose because
there's a new
one trying
to grow
underneath.
If we take
that old
dragon out,
there will be
room for the
new tooth
to grow!"

"NOOOOO!"
Sara roared.
She stomped
her feet
and crashed
into the
wastebasket.

Out spilled an
empty cereal box,
an egg carton,
two juice cans,
and a pasta box.

Sara scooped them
all up and took them
out to the garage.
There she found other
things she needed.

Sara cut

and glued

and taped

and painted.

She
made
ears,

and
a tail,

and
claws,

and very,
very
big
teeth.

Her dragon was finished.

But the dragon
looked sad.
His tooth hurt, too.

"Help me clean up,"
said Sara.
"Then you won't
think about
your tooth."

The dragon
looked even sadder.

"Okay, Dragon," said Sara.
"That tooth has to
come out. It hurts
because the new one
growing under it
needs more room!
Now . . . open your mouth!"

The dragon
opened his mouth.
Sara reached in and
gently pulled out a
big egg-carton tooth.

"There!" said Sara.
"All better!"
The dragon smiled.

Papa came in.
"How's the old
dragon tooth?"
he asked.

"All better," said Sara.
"Almost," she added,
and opened
her mouth wide.

Papa came in.
"How's the old
dragon tooth?"
he asked.

"All better," said Sara.
"Almost," she added,
and opened
her mouth wide.

Papa gently
pulled out
Sara's tooth.
Sure enough—
she felt better.

Sara smiled at
her dragon.

"Now," said Sara,
"we can watch our
new teeth grow!"

The
End